This book belongs to:

_____

William

Mummy

For Will, Polly and Bea

First published in Great Britain in 2018 by Andersen Press Ltd.,
20 Vauxhall Bridge Road, London SW1V 2SA.
Copyright © Eve Coy 2018.
The right of Eve Coy to be identified as the author and
illustrator of this work have been asserted by her in accordance
with the Copyright, Designs and Patents Act, 1988.
Printed and bound in China.
First edition.
British Library Cataloguing in Publication Data available.
ISBN 978-1-78344-541-7

Looking After William

Eve Coy

Andersen Press

This is my little boy, William.

Today, I'm his mummy.

William likes to get up early.

And dance and sing.

I get William ready,

then I make his
favourite breakfast.

William is full of energy
and needs lots of exercise.

Looking after William keeps me busy.

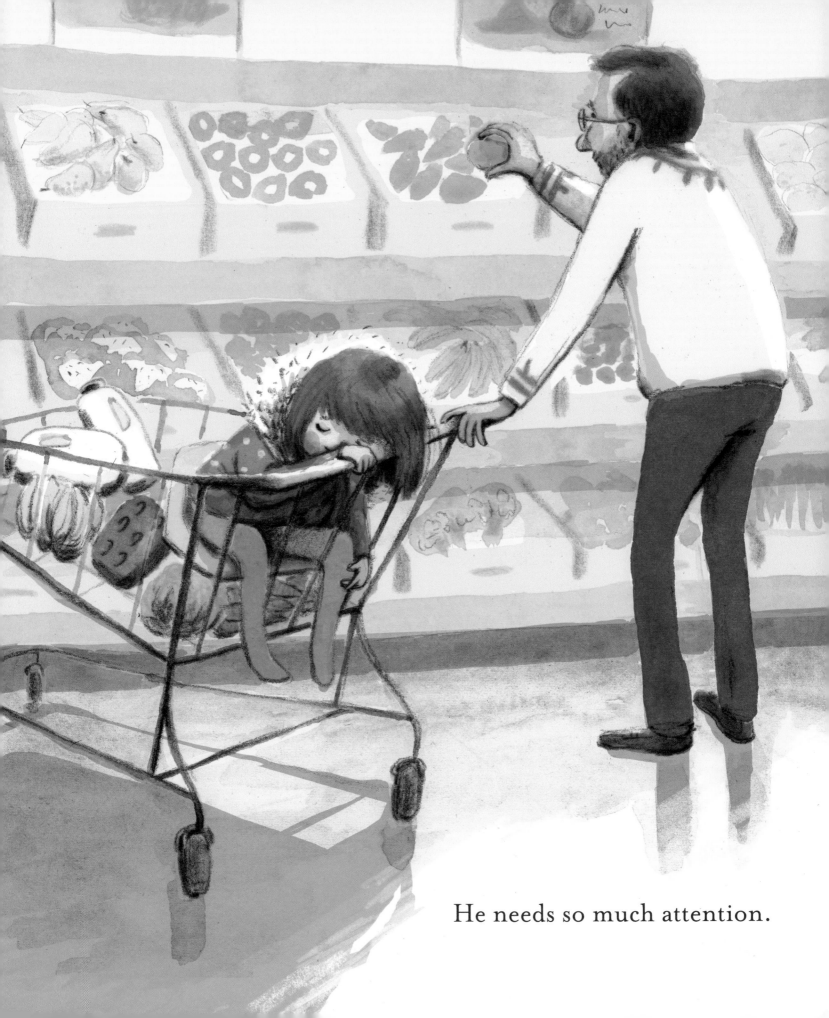

He needs so much attention.

Which can be tricky, because I have lots of jobs to do.

And he doesn't
always look where
he's going.

Sometimes, he just needs a little rest.

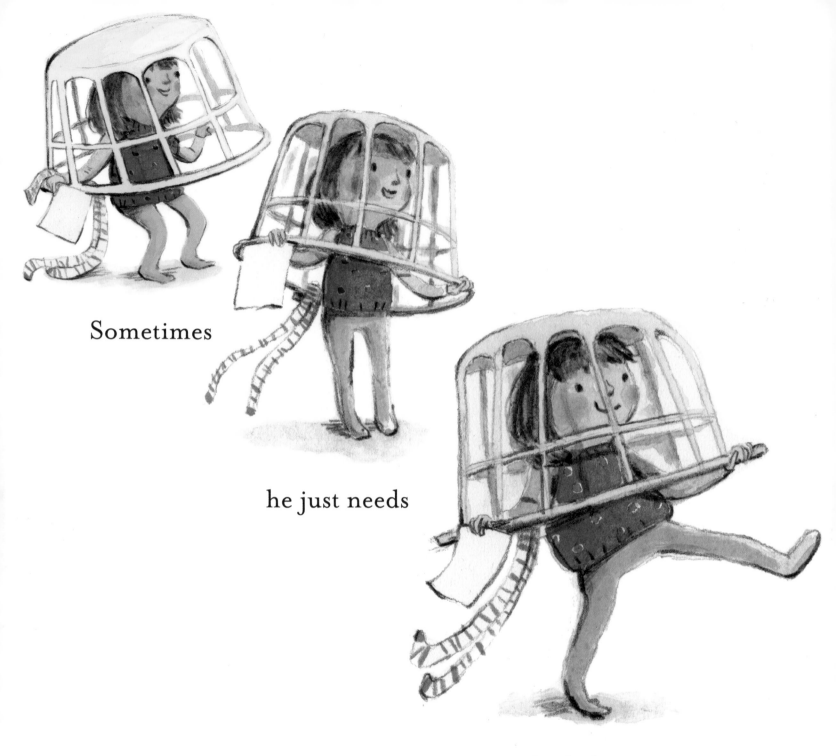

Sometimes

he just needs

a little love.

William is very clever.
I tell him he could do anything
when he grows up.

He could be
a lion tamer

or an astronaut.

He could be a famous chocolate maker.

A clever detective on
the case of the missing
chocolates.

Or a nurse who treats children
who eat too much chocolate.

But William doesn't want
to be any of these.

He only wants to do one job,
that's always packed
with adventure.

Being my Dad.

And maybe an astronaut,
but only if we can all be astronauts too.